say something

BY PEGGY MOSS / ILLUSTRATED BY LEA LYON

"If you think you are too small to make a difference,
try sleeping in a room with a mosquito." African Proverb

TILBURY HOUSE  PUBLISHERS   GARDINER, MAINE

There's a kid in my school who gets picked on all the time.

I think he's sad.

I think he's sad because he keeps his head down
when he walks down the hall—

—and he hardly ever says hello.

I don't pick on him.

I feel sorry for him.

There's another kid in my school who gets teased.

He gets called names.

When he's moving through the halls, kids push him
and tell him he's slow.

I walk on the other side of the hall.
I don't say those things.

A girl who rides on my bus
always sits alone.

Sometimes kids throw things at her and call her names.

The girls who sit behind her laugh.

I don't laugh.

I don't say anything.

One day my friends were out, and I had to sit

alone in the cafeteria.

Some kids came over to me and they started telling jokes.

I laughed until the jokes started to be about me.

My face burned. I looked down at the table.

I sat on my hands to keep them from moving so much.

I tried not to cry, but it was hard not to cry,

and when they saw my face getting wet,

the kids started laughing.

I wished I could stop crying.

I wished I could disappear.

When the kids left, I looked around the cafeteria.

I was surprised to see that the cafeteria was full of students.

There were even kids I knew, sitting at the table

right next to mine.

They were looking at me.
I could tell they
felt sorry for me.

When I went home, I told my big brother
I was mad at the kids at the table next to mine.

He shrugged and said, "Why? They didn't do anything."

"Right," I said.

On the bus the next day,
I sat next to the girl who
always sits alone.

She's really funny!

Do you think **YOU** can make a difference **?**

"I don't really care

what words they use—

I just want someone

to speak up

and make the teasing

stop!"

Sixth Grade Boy

Say something! Like what?

Students everywhere are stepping up to say, "That's not cool!" when other kids bully in school. And their words are making a world of difference.
Choose your own way to say, "I don't want to hear that!"
Then, practice, practice, practice!
Keep your goal in mind: make the teasing stop! Remember, humor works, but teasing back does not.

When you see someone else being teased, try these:

• Say something to the person who is getting teased. It doesn't matter what you say, really. Just saying "Hi" to someone you don't usually hang out with works. So does, "Come play on our team." Or, "Can I sit with you at lunch today?"

• Say something to the bully. Don't become part of the fight. But remember, often just a quick word or two will make the teasing or the mean-spirited joke stop. Every one of us has our own way of saying, "I don't want to hear that." Try: "Knock it off...." "Cut it out...." "That's so ten minutes ago!" "Oh, nice one." Or, "Yeah, that's cool." Or, "Grow up."

• Tell an adult—a parent, teacher, principal, school nurse, or someone else you trust. When teasing changes to pushing or feels scary, it's important for you to let someone know, before anyone gets hurt.

Why speak up?

• Because you can make teasing UN-cool. Most bullies tease because they want YOU to think they are cool. But teasing isn't cool. It's mean. If you don't laugh when a bully makes a joke about another kid, the joke is over. And when that happens, you've made a huge difference.

• If you don't, who will? When no one steps up to stop the teasing, the bullies get bolder, and often someone gets hurt.

• Because teasing will happen to you. (It happens to all of us.) You're going to want someone to speak up for you. So—show them how it's done.

YOU can !

If you are being bullied, speak up!

Things to say are: "Please stop." "That hurts my feelings." "I haven't done anything to you." Don't be afraid to tell an adult!

Want to find out more?

Check out these organizations and their websites:

- The Center for the Prevention of Hate Violence
  For information on what to do about bullying and to learn more about this book.
  www.preventinghate.org
- Partners Against Hate
  This organization offers promising education and counterracism strategies for youth and community professionals to fight prejudice and bigotry.
  www.Partnersagainsthate.org
- The Giraffe Project
  If you want inspiration about people with the courage to stick their necks out for the common good, visit this site. www.giraffe.org
- Kids' Quest
  This site will help you understand more about kids with health problems or disabilities. www.cdc.gov/ncbddd/kids

Want to do more?

- Bring a speaker to your school.

- Start a school anti-bullying campaign. There are many new and different programs being developed for school-based approaches. A good place to start is Don't Laugh at Me. Originally a song and then a book by Steve Seskin and now a program run by Peter Yarrow of Peter, Paul, and Mary fame, Operation Respect is free and has been used in thousands of schools. www.operationrespect.org

Remember YOU are the very best person to bring a change to your school.

"One person

speaking up

makes more noise

than a thousand people

who remain silent."

Thom Harnett,

Civil Rights Attorney

TILBURY HOUSE, PUBLISHERS
103 Brunswick Avenue, Gardiner, Maine 04345
800–582–1899 • www.tilburyhouse.com

First hardcover printing: May 2004 • 10 9 8 7 6 5
Firt paperback printing: August 2008 • 10 9 8 7 6 5 4 3

Dedications
For the kids who get teased, because you are not alone. And for the kids who speak up, because you make all the difference. And for Teddy. —PM

For Joni, Carlie, and Bernie —LL

Acknowledgments
Thank you to Steve Wessler for the chance, Betsy Sweet for the nudge, and Audrey, Jennifer, and Lea for giving the words life. Thanks to Paula and Ted Moss, who taught us to speak up. And thank you, John Beebe, for everything. —PM

My thanks to Ms. Jensen's seventh grade class at John Muir Middle School in San Leandro, California, Mr. Chapnick's fifth grade class at Lorin Eden School in Hayward, California, the fifth grade summer day camp group at the Richmond YMCA in California, and, especially, Cameron, my narrator. I couldn't have illustrated this book without you. —LL

Library of Congress Cataloging-in-Publication Data

Moss, Peggy, 1966-
   Say something / Peggy Moss ; illustrated by Lea Lyon.-- 1st ed.
        p. cm.
Summary: A child who never says anything when other children are being teased or bullied finds herself in their position one day when jokes are made at her expense and no one speaks up.
   ISBN 0-88448-261-8 (Hardcover : alk. paper)
   [1. Bullies--Fiction. 2. Assertiveness (Psychology)--Fiction. 3. Schools--Fiction.]
I. Lyon, Lea, 1945- ill. II. Title.
   PZ7.M85357Say 2004
   [E]--dc22
                                        2003023759

Designed by Geraldine Millham, Westport, MA.
Printed by Sung In Printing Ltd., Dang Jung-Dong 242-2, GunPo-si, Kyunggi-do, Korea; January 2011.